# Three's a Crowd

by

## Jo Cotterill

## Illustrated by Jen Collins

First published in 2012 in Great Britain by
Barrington Stoke Ltd
18 Walker St, Edinburgh, EH3 7LP

www.barringtonstoke.co.uk

ISBN: 978-1-78112-006-4

Printed in China by Leo

# Contents

# Chapter 1
# Two Dates!

My best mate Ben looked at me.

"They *both* asked you out?" he said. "Are you sure, Molly?"

"Of course I am," I said. "I'm so happy! It feels a bit like a dream."

"Hang on ..." Ben sat down beside me. It was lunch time at school and we were outside. "So Oliver came over ..." Ben began.

"No," I said. "He sent me a note. It was in my locker this morning."

"What did it say?" Ben asked.

"It was so cute," I told him. "It said, *You have my heart*, with a little picture of a heart. And then on the other side it said, *Will you go out with me? From Oliver.* So I wrote back and said I would."

"You said yes?" asked Ben.

"Well, he's so sweet," I told him. "He always holds the door open for me. And tells me I have pretty eyes."

"Right," Ben said. He gave me an odd look.

"And then in Maths," I went on, "the teacher was late, and Jack came over to me. He wanted to tell me all about his weekend. You know he's in a band?"

Ben nodded. "Yeah, I know."

"Well," I said, "he asked me to go and hear them play! Just me! And then the two of us can go for dinner. Isn't that cool!"

"But, Molly, you said you'd go out with Oliver," Ben reminded me.

"That was before Jack asked me!" I said. "I couldn't say no to Jack, could I?"

"So ..." Ben took a book out of his bag, "now you're going out with both Oliver *and* Jack?"

"Why not?" I asked. "I mean, it's not like ..." I stopped. "What are you trying to say? Don't you think I should?"

"No, no." Ben opened his book. "If you want to go out with them, you go out with them. Have a good time."

I didn't understand. Why was Ben being so weird about this?

# Chapter 2
# Super-sweet Oliver

"Here we are," said Oliver, as he held the door open for me.

"Thanks," I said.  We were at the cinema. Oliver let me choose the film, which was nice of him.

"I'll get the tickets," he said. "Do you want pop-corn?"

"Yes please."

"You look really pretty today, Molly," he said. Then his face went red. "I mean, you always look pretty."

Now I was going red too! "Thanks," I said, feeling pleased.

Oliver let me pick where to sit in the cinema. Then he held my bag while I sat down. He was so sweet!

I liked the film a lot, but I did worry about Oliver. He didn't try to put his arm around me at all! And yet I knew he liked me. I put my hand on top of his at one point, and he did hold my hand back. But after a bit it got kind of hot, and I needed that hand for the pop-corn.

When the film ended, Oliver looked at me and said, "You want to get a pizza?"

So we went to the pizza place and he pulled out my chair for me. "You're very polite," I said.

He looked surprised. "Am I?"

"You hold doors open for me and stuff."

"That's because I like you." He looked at me. "I like you a lot, Molly. I think you're pretty. And funny and kind."

I didn't know what to say. "Wow," I said, after a second. "Thanks."

"I want to know everything about you," he said.

"Like what?"

"What colour do you like best?" he asked.

"Pink."

He smiled. "OK. What ... er ... food do you like best?"

"Pizza." I smiled too.

He smiled back again. He did have a very sweet smile. His hair was soft and brown and fell over his eyes. "So you like pink and pizza," he said.

"Not pink pizza," I said. "That would be disgusting!"

"Let me ask another one ..."

Oliver was easy to talk to. He liked to listen to me, which was nice. Lots of boys don't listen, but Oliver did. He wanted to know how I felt about school, friends, my dancing – everything. "Dancing is cool," he said. "I'd like to come and see you dance."

"I'm in a show soon," I said. "I've got a big solo in it."

"Then I must come! Tell me when it is."

When we had eaten our pizzas, it was time to go. "I had a great time," I told him.

He smiled. "Me too. Can we do it again?"

I was about to say, 'yes', but then I remembered I had a date with Jack. Maybe I should tell Jack I didn't want to go out with him after all?

No. I would go out with Jack, and then I'd choose which boy I liked more. That

15

would be fair. "I'll let you know," I said to Oliver.

He looked sad. "That means 'no'," he said.

"No, it doesn't," I told him. "I really like you. It's just that I'm going to think about it first."

"OK." He kissed me on the cheek. "See you."

I went home with a smile on my face. Oliver would be the perfect boyfriend!

# Chapter 3
# Ben Makes Trouble

"So you want to go out with Oliver again," said my mate Ben. We were sitting on our bench outside school.

I smiled. "He was so sweet! He asked me all about myself. He wanted to know everything. He really listened to me."

Ben nodded. "That's good. So he knows all about you now."

"Totally," I said. "And he gets me, you know? He understands me."

"What about him?" Ben asked.

"What do you mean?"

"What did you find out about him?" Ben asked. "I mean, if he asked you all this stuff about what you like ... did you find out what *he* likes?"

"Well," I said, "he likes ... er ..." I stopped. "I don't know. The same things I like, I suppose."

"Didn't he say?"

"No," I said, "not so much. I told him what I liked, and he agreed." I gave a frown. "Now that I look back ..."

"He spent the whole evening saying how sweet and pretty you were," said Ben. "But he didn't say anything about himself at all. Isn't that a bit weird?"

"No," I said. I felt like I had to stand up for Oliver. "He was being sensitive. He wanted to make me happy."

Ben looked away. "That's all very well," he said, "but do you really want a boyfriend who just agrees with you all the time? He sounds a bit boring to me."

I was cross. "He's not boring! He's lovely. I *like* the fact that he doesn't talk about himself all the time!"

Ben held up his hands. "All right, all right!" he said. "I was just saying..."

"Well, don't." I was in a mood now. What did Ben know about it anyway? It wasn't like *he* was my boyfriend. What right did he have to be so mean about Oliver? Oliver was just the kind and caring sort, that's all. He wanted to make me happy. That was a *good* thing, right?

So why was I feeling all weird about him now?

# Chapter 4
# Super-cool Jack

Two days later, I went to hear Jack's band play. It was only a practice, but they were amazing! I had no idea Jack had such a fab voice! He kept looking at me while he was singing, and it made me blush. When they were finished, I went over to him.

"That was the best thing ever," I told him.

Jack grinned. "Thanks. We've been practising hard. We're going to enter a competition."

"Wow," I said. "What's the prize?"

"A record contract!" said Jack. "It would be the start of my career!"

"Wow!" It sounded great to me. "You mean, they'd play your songs on the radio?"

"Yeah – and we'd get to play gigs and do interviews and stuff," Jack told me.

I smiled. "I bet you'll win! You're amazing."

"Thanks," Jack said, and put his arm around me. "Come on. Let's go get a burger."

"Don't you have to help clear up?" I asked. The other boys in the band were putting away the drums and other stuff.

"Nah," said Jack. "Not today. I'm going out with you!"

I felt like I was on a date with a pop star! Jack was amazing – so good-looking and confident. He had short blond hair and his eyes were deep blue. When we went into the burger place, three girls turned round to look at him. I felt so proud that I was his date!

"This place isn't as big as the one in New York," said Jack, "but it'll do."

"You've been to New York?" I asked.

"Yeah. It was so cool. You know the Empire State Building? We went up it at night. You could see all the lights of the city."

"Dreamy," I said.

"If it's lights you like," Jack said, "the rainforest is the best place."

"Rainforest?" I asked.

"Yeah," Jack said. "There are these tiny bugs that glow in the dark. And when you're

in your tent at night, you can see them outside. Little lights flying around."

"When did you go to the rainforest?" I asked. My burger and chips were getting cold, but I didn't want to miss a word.

Jack gave a shrug. "Two years ago. My dad took me and my sister. She didn't like it. Kept going on about spiders and snakes. What a pain!"

He said it like spiders and snakes were no problem at all! He was just – wow. So cool. Like a celebrity. "Where else have you been?" I asked.

"Oh, nowhere much," he said. "Some places in Italy. And Florida, a couple of times. My dad knows someone who works in Hollywood too, so we went there last summer."

"Hollywood?" I felt like I would pass out with excitement.

Jack laughed. "Yeah, it was so funny. They were shooting a film when we got there. And someone hadn't turned up, so I had to get into this costume and be in the scene! It was mad."

"You were in a Hollywood film?"

"Well, I don't know if my scene is still there," he said. "They cut out a lot before the final film comes out." He looked down. "Don't you want your fries?"

I wasn't hungry any more. Jack was *so* the boy for me!

# Chapter 5
# Oliver or Jack?

"So now you want Jack as your boyfriend," said Ben.

"Yes," I said.

"Jack, not Oliver."

"Jack's so cool!" I said. "He's done all this amazing stuff. Did you know he's been to New York? And the rainforest. *And* he's been in a Hollywood film!"

"Mmm."

"What do you mean, 'mmm'?" I asked. I was cross with Ben now. "What's your problem with Jack?"

"Nothing, nothing." Ben looked shifty. "But ... are you sure it's all true?"

"What's all true?"

"That Jack's been to New York, and in a film, and all that?"

I gave him an angry look. "Why would he lie?"

"To impress you."

"Jack's not like that," I said. "Some people are just cool. They just have *something*. He doesn't need to try to impress me. He's just *Jack*."

Ben let out a sigh. "So you're going to tell Oliver you don't want to see him again?"

"Yes ..." I said. I did feel a bit bad about it. "Oh, I don't know! He's so nice. I don't want to hurt him."

"But you can't go out with both of them." Ben said.

"I know." I looked at him. "You're my best mate, Ben. You know me better than anyone. Which one do *you* think is right for me?"

Ben didn't say anything for a moment but there was something funny in the way he looked at me. "I can't choose for you," he said at last. "You have to choose for yourself."

"That's no help!" I moaned. "Come on, Ben, you're my mate."

"OK," he said. He still had that funny look in his eyes. "Let's talk about them both. Oliver is nice and kind, and he's a good listener."

"Very important in a boyfriend," I said.

Ben nodded. "I agree. But he doesn't seem very interesting. He doesn't have anything to say for himself. What do you like about him? Apart from the fact that he's kind?"

"Er ..." My mind was blank. "I don't know."

"OK," said Ben. "Let's talk about Jack."

I smiled. "He's so cool! He rocks!"

"Is he kind?" asked Ben. "Did he listen to you?"

"Well, no," I said. "But that's because he was telling me all about himself ..."

"Sounds like he's a bit of a show-off, if you ask me," said Ben.

All of a sudden, I was cross again. "You're doing this on purpose, Ben! You just want to put me off Jack. I'd be the coolest girl in school if I went out with him!"

"Is that what matters to you?" Ben asked.

"Yes," I said. "I mean – no! You're messing with my head!" I stood up. "I know what this is, Ben. You don't want me to have a boyfriend! Anyone would think you were jealous!"

Ben stood up too. His face was pale. "Well, maybe I am!"

# Chapter 6
# A Big Shock!

I looked at Ben. His hair was all sticking up at the front. His eyes had that funny look in them again, and it felt like they were burning into me. "You what?" I said in a small voice.

"Maybe I am jealous!" he said again. "Maybe I don't like watching you go out with other boys. Maybe I've been waiting for you for a long time – for you to see ..." He stopped. "Oh, it doesn't matter. Forget it."

"No," I said. "No – tell me. What do you mean, 'waiting for me'? You're my mate. Aren't you? Ben, what are you trying to say?"

He looked at me again, and his eyes were soft. "Maybe I don't want to be just your mate any more, Molly. Can't you see I'm crazy about you?"

"Oh!" I didn't know what to say. "Ben, I ..."

We were silent for a moment. My head was in a spin. Ben – my best mate, my oldest friend – was crazy about me!

Oliver was sweet and kind but he was a bit boring.

Jack was cool and amazing but he only cared about himself.

And Ben ... Ben was everything, wasn't he? He was smart and sweet and funny and kind and interesting.

Why had I never seen it before?

"Oh," I said again. "Wow. I mean ..."

"Molly," said Ben, "I know it's a bit of a shock. I'm not Oliver, and I'm not Jack – but I like you so much. And I wanted to ask you out a long time ago, but I didn't dare. You don't have to say anything. I'm glad I've told you." He smiled, and it was such a beautiful smile. It made my heart skip a beat.

I smiled back. "I'm glad you've told me too." All of a sudden, I felt shy. "Maybe ... maybe we could go out on a date."

"Yeah?" His eyes shone. "You think?"

I blushed. "Just to see what it was like."

"Cool.  Molly ..." He bit his lip.  "Can I kiss you?  Just to see what it's like ..."

"Oh.  Well, I suppose so ..."

He leaned towards me and I closed my eyes.

Oliver – Jack – Ben.  Who needs three boys when you can have one perfect boyfriend?

*Also by* **JO COTTERILL**...

# TAKE TWO

One prom + One hot boy + Two best friends
= A lot of trouble!

Max asks Carla *and* her best friend Lily to the
prom. Instead of getting mad, they decide to get
*even*. It's sure to be a night Max will never forget!

www.barringtonstoke.co.uk

*And...*

# LOVE BITES

Grace loves James. James loves Grace.
So far, so good.

But James doesn't know that Grace has a dark
secret. Maybe telling him the truth is the worst
thing Grace could do...

www.barringtonstoke.co.uk